D1294294

Donna O'Neeshuck
Was Chased By Some Cows

Donna O'Neeshuck Was Chased By Some Cows

by Bill Grossman • illustrated by Sue Truesdell

Harper & Row, Publishers

Library of Congress Cataloging-in-Publication Data
Grossman, Bill.
    Donna O'Neeshuck was chased by some cows.

    Summary: Donna O'Neeshuck cannot understand why
she is being chased by cows, mooses, gooses, and a
host of others, until she discovers that her head pats
are irresistible.
    [1. Animals—Fiction.   2. Stories in rhyme]
I. Truesdell, Sue, ill.   II. Title.
PZ8.3.G914Do 1988   [E]   85-45823
ISBN 0-06-022158-5
ISBN 0-06-022159-3 (lib. bdg.)

1   2   3   4   5   6   7   8   9   10
First Edition

To my father,
George Grossman,
whose pats on the
head are greatly missed.

B.G.

For Joe

S.T.

Donna O'Neeshuck
Was Chased By Some Cows

Donna O'Neeshuck was chased by some cows,

And also by mooses and gooses and sows.

It happened one day

When Donna at play

Patted a cow on the head.

The cow got her friends and they started to chase
Poor Donna O'Neeshuck all over the place.
They chased her through farms,
Through pastures and barns—
Around and around and around.

She ran down the street past a uniformed cop.

He blew on his whistle and made them all stop.

"Thank you," she said,

And she patted his head—

And the cop started chasing her too.

They chased her up roads full of buses and trucks.

They chased her down rivers all covered with ducks.

They chased her on bridges

And ledges and ridges—

Around and around and around.

The voice of a cat in a treetop above her
Said, "Quickly, young lady! Come here and take cover.
Climb up here with me."
So she climbed up his tree
And thanked him and patted his head.

But the cat chased her too, so she quickly climbed down.
The others joined in when she got to the ground.

She barely was racing
Ahead of their chasing
When a boy pedaled by on a bike.

He slammed on his brakes, and he jumped off his bike.
"Here," said the boy, "take my bike if you like."
"Thank you," she said,
Patting his head—
But he hopped on his bike, and he chased her.

They chased her past chickens and turkeys and birds,
Through bunches of buffalo running in herds,
Past foxes and bears
Eating apples and pears—
Around and around and around.

She yelled to a horse with a pack on his back,
"Oh, please let me ride on your back in your pack."
"Sure," the horse said.
So she patted his head—
And the horse started chasing her too.

They chased her up sidewalks. They chased her down streets.

They chased her through gardens of carrots and beets,

Through windows and doors

Of houses and stores—

Till she stumbled right into a doctor.

The cows and the mooses crashed into the doctor,
Who bumped into Donna O'Neeshuck and knocked her
Right through a wall.

And the rest of them all
Went charging along close behind her.

They chased her up mountains. They chased her down valleys.

They chased her up highways. They chased her down alleys.

They chased her for hours
Through bushes and flowers—
Around and around and around.

She ran and she ran just as far as one can.

Then she slowed, and she stopped, and she threw up her hands.

And she turned and stood facing
Those folks who were chasing
And said to them, *"What do you want?"*

"Head pats!" they said. "We want pats on the head.
You give such incredible head pats," they said.
"They're so awfully good,
We thought that it would
Be nice if you gave us some more."

She gave them five head pats. They begged her for ten.

She gave them ten head pats. They begged her again.

So she patted away

For most of the day....

Then she stopped and sat down and looked tired.

She said to them all, "Do you know what I'd like?"
Then the boy pedaled over to her on his bike,
And he patted her head.
"Thank you!" she said.

Then everyone patted each other.

Now, head pats from anyone always are nice.

But head pats from Donna O'Neeshuck are twice

As good as the rest.

Yep, hers are the best.

GCBA '89 - '90